WHEN THE MOON WEPT FIRE

A Celestial Fantasy Novel

By Deepali

Copyright Page

When the Moon Wept Fire

This is a work of fiction.

Names, characters, places, and incidents are products of the author's imagination.

Any resemblance to actual persons, living or dead, or actual events is purely coincidental.

First Edition, 2025

Cover Art: Deepali / AI Concept + Design

ISBN: 978-93-344-2029-6

For inquiries:

Email: lotus.sutras.info@gmail.com

Website: lotussutrabooks.com

Dedication Page

To the moonlit dreams that never left me,

and to the fire that taught me to rise.

— Deepali

Epigraph

"Even the moon must break before it can shine."

— Celestial Proverb

Acknowledgments

You can include this at the front or end of the book.

Acknowledgments

My deepest gratitude to every reader who believes in magic, destiny, and the power of stories. You make this journey radiant.

Special thanks to those who supported this book from its earliest spark to its final page.

TABLE OF CONTENTS

Prologue – The White Tiger's Prophecy

The night sky burned with a rare crimson aurora, streaking across the heavens like molten rivers. In the quiet palace of the Moon Empress, a shadow moved with silent grace.

The White Tiger emerged, its fur glimmering like frost under moonlight, eyes molten amber, fixed on the Empress. Each step it took left ghostly echoes on the polished silver floor.

"You know why I come," the creature intoned, voice deep and resonant, vibrating through the marble halls.

Moon Empress Liuyin's hands trembled ever so slightly as she clutched the silver crescent staff. "I do," she whispered. "I have seen the threads... the child... the fate that wavers."

The Tiger's gaze pierced her. "Rebirth or ruin. The child born under your care holds the world in balance. One wrong move, and the heavens themselves will tremble."

The Empress bowed her head, swallowing the lump in her throat. She knew the cost—erasing the child from the mortal record, sealing powers, hiding her in a distant village, severing her from all memory of the Moon Realm. A mother's love bound her decision, yet duty demanded cruelty.

"You will hide her," the Tiger said, tail coiling with quiet menace. "The Sun Lord's eyes are everywhere. Only secrecy can grant her life. And only the seed of love—unexpected, untested—will guide her through the shadows that come."

The Empress's breath hitched. "And the curse?" she asked softly. "Will it reach her?"

The Tiger's amber eyes darkened. "The Black Lotus festers where jealousy takes root. Its petals will stain the lands she may love. She will lose her senses one by one. Only one who dares walk beyond law, beyond duty, will stand beside her."

A faint chill ran through the Empress. "I... I will do what must be done."

The Tiger inclined its massive head. "Then the threads are set. Watch the heavens, Empress. For destiny is neither kind nor cruel—it simply comes. And when the moon weeps fire, all will be revealed."

A gust of wind from the open balcony scattered silver petals across the room. The Tiger disappeared into shadow, leaving only the whisper of prophecy, the faint scent of jasmine, and a world poised on the edge of calamity and hope.

Moonlight fell on the Empress's face as she whispered the name she had erased from every record: *Selunara.*

She was both promise and peril, the child who would shape the future—and no mortal, not even her mother, could foresee how the threads would unravel.

Chapter 1 –

The Child at the Door

The storm had passed, leaving the village wrapped in a heavy, silvery mist. Lanterns flickered along the cobblestone streets, casting long shadows that danced with the wind. The first hints of dawn painted the sky in pale apricot and violet streaks, but the village felt suspended, waiting.

At the edge of the village, on the threshold of a small, unremarkable home, a glowing cradle sat under the eaves. Moonlight pooled over it, bathing the infant in ethereal light. No one had left a note, no one had knocked—yet the child was placed with care, as if guided by unseen hands.

Iryndor, the village healer, was the first to notice. Kneeling beside the cradle, he adjusted the soft blanket, his rough hands trembling. "By the spirits..." he whispered. The child's skin glimmered faintly, and between her delicate eyebrows was a tiny mark shaped like a lotus, faint but unmistakable.

"She... she isn't like other children," Iryndor muttered, awe mingling with fear. The lotus mark pulsed once, faintly glowing, as though recognizing him.

From the shadows, a whisper of silver robes appeared. The Moon Empress, disguised in mortal form, observed silently. Her face was pale, eyes soft yet distant, reflecting both love and the weight of impossible choices. She had given the command, and yet watching her daughter—her Selunara— placed in mortal hands tore at her heart.

A soft wind carried the scent of jasmine, a lingering trace of the Moon Palace's magic. The Empress's lips moved in silent prayer. *Grow strong, little one. Survive, and remember only what you must when the time comes.*

The villagers, drawn by the light, gathered cautiously. Some crossed themselves, muttering prayers. Others merely stared, sensing something beyond the ordinary. The child cooed, eyes fluttering open for the first time, reflecting the dawn sky with a brilliance that seemed almost otherworldly. Iryndor picked her up carefully, cradling her to his chest. "We must protect her," he murmured, glancing around the quiet streets. "Whoever left her... or whatever sent her... she is no ordinary child."

The Empress took a step forward, invisible to the others, and placed a hand over her heart. The faint glow of the lotus mark responded, pulsing once more as if acknowledging its mother's presence. A single tear slipped down her cheek.

This child will bear the weight of worlds, the Empress thought, *and she will choose love or destruction. May the Moon guide her steps, for the path ahead is shadowed and bright alike.*

With one last glance at the glowing infant, the Empress vanished into the silver mist, leaving Selunara in mortal hands. The village had no idea they were now guardians of the future.

And in the silent dawn, the first threads of destiny began to weave themselves around the child who would one day be both savior and storm.

Chapter 2 – The Birthmark Fades

Selunara grew quietly in the village, her presence a delicate ripple against the ordinary life around her. By day she ran through dew-soaked fields, chased by the laughter of other children; by night, she stared into the silvered sky, feeling the stirrings of something she could not name.

It was on one such night, as moonlight spilled across her wooden window, that she noticed it. Between her eyebrows, the faint lotus mark shimmered ever so slightly, barely perceptible, as though waking from a long slumber. She touched it with a trembling finger.

"What... am I?" she whispered into the stillness, heart fluttering with a mixture of fear and wonder.

Iryndor, who had been watching from the doorway, stepped closer. "That mark," he said softly, "is older than you think, Selunara. It is part of who you are... part of something far greater than this village."

Her eyes widened. "Something greater?"

"Destiny," he said, hesitating. "Or... a burden. Some marks carry light, some shadow. Yours... will reveal itself when the time comes."

Even as he spoke, a flicker of shadow passed in the corner of her vision, a whisper of movement she could not quite identify. Her pulse quickened. *Am I being watched?*

Over the following weeks, the lotus mark became more noticeable, pulsing faintly at certain times—the moon's rise, moments of heightened emotion, and once, inexplicably, in the presence of a stranger she had not yet met. Each pulse carried warmth and faint resonance, as if the mark itself had a heartbeat.

The villagers noticed too. Some stared a little too long; others whispered of the "moon child," a child touched by the heavens. But none could see the faint glow, the secret embedded in her skin, the subtle pulse that linked her to something far beyond the mortal realm.

Selunara's nights were filled with dreams. Shadows shaped like tigers and flames moved in patterns she did not understand. Sometimes she awoke with tears staining her cheeks, or a sudden ache in her chest, fleeting but intense. The lotus mark pulsed in answer, as if trying to comfort her, or perhaps guide her.

Iryndor continued to watch her quietly, guarding her with unwavering devotion. He often sat by her bedside, whispering tales of healers, celestial beings, and distant realms, careful to avoid truths that could frighten her. Yet, he could not hide the feeling that the world was already shifting around the girl. Every fading mark, every pulse of light, was a herald of change.

One evening, as the sun dipped below distant hills, painting the sky in molten gold and violet, Selunara caught sight of her reflection in the village well. The lotus mark shimmered more brightly than ever before, a soft glow that reached toward the fading light. For a moment, she felt a strange connection—something old, ancient, and infinitely powerful—stirring deep within her.

A whisper echoed in her mind, faint but certain: *You are not alone. The world awaits your choice.*

Her breath caught. She did not yet know what the choice would be, or what darkness would come to test her. But as she traced the glowing lotus with her finger, she understood one undeniable truth: she could not remain the ordinary girl the village believed her to be. The mark was fading, yes—but in its fading lay the first pulse of awakening, and the first hint of the extraordinary life she had yet to embrace.

Outside, the wind shifted, carrying the faint scent of jasmine and something darker, a whisper of shadow that had been watching, waiting. Somewhere beyond the hills, destiny moved, unseen yet inevitable, threading Selunara's life toward a path that would shake the heavens themselves.

✦ ☾ ✦

Chapter 3

The Dreaming Lotus

The village slept beneath a blanket of silver moonlight, but Selunara's mind could not find rest. Shadows shifted across her small room, cast by the flickering lantern on the wooden wall, and outside, the wind carried a faint, almost imperceptible hum.

It began as a dream, or perhaps a memory she had not lived yet. She stood in a luminous glade, mist curling around ancient trees. The moon hovered impossibly close, bathing the ground in soft silver, and from the mist emerged a creature both terrifying and magnificent—a white tiger, its fur shimmering like frost, eyes molten amber.

"You are awake, child of the Moon," the Tiger intoned, voice deep, vibrating in her chest. "Your path is uncertain. Shadow and light entwine, and the balance will tremble. The choice is yours, though the cost is not yours alone to bear."

Selunara took a cautious step forward. Her fingers tingled, brushing against something unseen, and the lotus mark between her brows pulsed once, strong and warm. She gasped. The Tiger's gaze locked with hers, and for a heartbeat, she felt as if time itself had paused.

"Why... why me?" she whispered, voice trembling. "I'm just a village girl. I can't—"

"You are more," the Tiger interrupted, voice softer now but edged with steel. "And the world will know. The Black Lotus grows. Shadows seek to claim what should be protected. You will awaken, child, and each sense you rely upon may fail as you step closer to your destiny."

The ground beneath her feet seemed to ripple like water, silver light bending and twisting. She felt fear, yes, but also a strange exhilaration, a whisper of power she could almost grasp. The Tiger's tail swept across the mist, and in its wake, small petals shimmered—white lotus, fragile yet brilliant.

"Seek the one who walks in shadow yet guards the flame," it said. "He comes when the moon fades, and your paths will cross, though neither of you yet knows what binds you."

Selunara's heart skipped a beat. *A stranger? Who?* But before she could form the question aloud, the Tiger vanished, leaving only the rustle of leaves and the faint scent of jasmine.

She awoke with a start, breath ragged, palms pressed to her chest. The lotus mark glimmered faintly in the moonlight streaming through the window. She touched it, half expecting it to vanish like a dream—but it pulsed, slow and certain, as if affirming the truth of what she had seen.

Iryndor, who had been watching from the doorway, whispered softly, "Your dreams are not idle, Selunara. The

Tiger has come for you, even in shadow. Remember what it said, and remember... you are not alone."

Selunara's fingers lingered on the mark, warmth spreading through her fingertips. "I feel it," she murmured. "Something is coming... and I don't know if I'm ready."

But in the quiet of her room, under the silvered moon, she felt the first stirrings of courage. The mark was fading, yes—but each pulse was a heartbeat of awakening, a warning, and a promise.

Outside, the wind shifted again, carrying the faintest trace of shadow along with the lingering scent of moonlight. Somewhere in the darkness, unseen eyes watched. And Selunara, asleep yet wide awake in her dreams, had felt the first brush of destiny.

Chapter 4

The Stranger in the Market

The market bustled with the early morning crowd. The scent of fresh herbs mingled with the aroma of roasting sweetbreads, and children darted between stalls, laughing as merchants shouted their wares. Selunara navigated the throng with practiced ease, a basket of herbs in her hand, when movement at the edge of her vision caught her attention.

A boy, or perhaps a young man, stumbled from the shadows of an alley, colliding into her with startling force.

“Watch where you’re going!” Selunara snapped instinctively, though the basket tumbled to the ground, spilling its contents.

“I—I’m sorry,” the stranger stammered, catching himself. His dark, half-up hair tumbled over his shoulders, and his eyes, sharp yet unreadable, flicked to hers. There was something... not quite ordinary about him. A pull, subtle but insistent, tugged at her chest.

“You’re not from here,” she said, eyes narrowing.

“Perhaps,” he replied softly, voice smooth, careful, carrying a hidden weight. “I’ve lost my way.”

Selunara glanced at the herbs scattered across the cobblestones. “Then let me help you—careful, though, people will notice.” She bent to gather them, her fingers brushing against his for a fleeting instant. Heat radiated from his touch, though it was subtle, almost imperceptible.

The stranger watched her, expression unreadable, and for a moment the market seemed to fade, the voices of merchants and children dimming. Selunara felt an odd awareness, a ripple of something she could not name: a presence both familiar and strange.

“Iryndor!” she called suddenly, scanning the crowd. The healer appeared immediately, concern etched on his face. He gave the stranger a careful once-over before nodding ever so slightly at Selunara. He seemed... cautious, yet silently approving.

The stranger bowed lightly. “I mean no harm,” he said. There was an elegance in the way he moved, the kind born of careful training and hidden power. “I only seek... a place to rest.”

Selunara studied him, her intuition prickling. There was honesty in his tone, yes, but shadows lingered behind his eyes. Still, something in her chest urged her to trust him, or at least, not to push him away entirely.

“You can stay,” she said finally, offering a hand. “But only for a while. And I’ll be watching.”

He smiled faintly, almost imperceptibly, and the faintest pulse of warmth brushed the space between them. “I would expect nothing less.”

As the market returned to its lively rhythm, Selunara could not shake the feeling that destiny had just stepped closer. The lotus mark between her brows tingled, a quiet reminder of the path she could not yet see.

And somewhere, hidden beneath shadows and smoke of distant lands, unseen eyes watched the exchange, taking note of the girl and the stranger who had entered her life. A bond was forming, subtle, fragile—but it was enough to shift the currents of fate.

For Selunara, the world had grown larger in a single moment. And though she did not know it yet, the stranger would come to be both her protector and her greatest challenge.

Chapter 5

Hearth and Hellfire

Night fell with unnatural stillness, and the village seemed to hold its breath. Selunara, unaware of the shifting currents of power around her, sat by the hearth, mending a torn cloak. The firelight flickered across her features, casting soft shadows over the delicate curve of her lotus mark.

Outside, Aelthar moved silently, blending into darkness as if he were part of it. His presence was a ripple in the air, subtle yet undeniable. He traced the perimeter of the village, weaving faint lines of shadow and hellfire between buildings, creating protective wards that would only be visible to those who knew how to see them. The villagers were blissfully unaware, their safety ensured by a power they could neither perceive nor understand.

Aelthar paused atop a roof, his eyes scanning the distant hills where the first hints of dawn would soon appear. A stir in the celestial realm had reached the Sun Lord's attention. Orders had been issued, quiet and secretive: watch the girl. Keep her within reach. Do not let the prophecy unfold.

"The child awakens sooner than expected," Aelthar muttered under his breath, jaw tight. His hands clenched. Every pulse of Selunara's lotus mark resonated with him, reminding him of the vow he had sworn: to protect her at any cost. Even if it meant defying the laws of heaven itself.

In the Celestial Hall, the Sun Lord, radiant and imperious, leaned over a polished golden map. His fingers traced the lands, stopping where the mortal village lay hidden beneath ordinary roofs. "She stirs," he said, voice sharp as sunlight. "And the Moon hides her too well. Increase surveillance. The smallest error could let her powers bloom unchecked."

Back in the village, Selunara shivered as a strange warmth brushed her skin, as if invisible hands shielded her from unseen danger. The fire flickered violently, then calmed. Her lotus mark pulsed softly, a silent reminder that forces beyond her comprehension were now converging.

Aelthar returned to the shadows, watching her through the latticed window. He had risked exposure several times already, bending rules he would one day pay for. Yet with each heartbeat, each flicker of the mark, he felt the tether between them grow stronger. The world outside might not understand the threat, but he did. And he would not fail.

The night stretched on, heavy with anticipation. Somewhere beyond the hills, the Sun Lord's watchers moved, their eyes cold, precise. And yet, the wards of shadow and fire held firm, shielding the village, shielding Selunara.

Selunara yawned, finally settling by the hearth, oblivious to the peril that swirled around her. The warmth of the fire and the quiet comfort of home belied the storm that had begun to stir in the realms above. But her lotus mark, faintly glowing in the hearthlight, was a beacon. It was a warning. And in time, she would understand both its power and its peril.

Aelthar melted into the darkness once more, leaving only the faintest trace of warmth behind, as if the shadow itself whispered a promise: *I will protect you. No matter the cost.*

Chapter 6

The Dark Omen at the Lake

The Sacred Lake had always been a place of calm and reflection. Its waters mirrored the moon so perfectly that villagers often whispered the lake was a second sky, a piece of heaven resting upon the earth. Selunara, drawn by habit and a strange inner pull, wandered there one evening, carrying a small lantern and a basket of herbs.

But tonight, the reflection was wrong.

The surface of the water rippled unnaturally, dark veins twisting through the silver light. A cold wind rose without warning, bending the reeds and stirring the surface into ripples that distorted the moon's reflection. Selunara froze, sensing the unease before fully understanding it.

"Something is wrong," she whispered, her breath fogging in the night air. The lotus mark between her eyebrows pulsed faintly, warm against her skin, as if warning her.

Suddenly, the water shimmered and shifted, and she saw shapes moving beneath the surface—long, twisting shadows, almost alive. Fear surged, but so did an inexplicable draw, as if the lake itself was calling her to witness the corruption.

A voice broke the silence, low and steady. "Do not step too close."

Selunara spun, and there, at the edge of the reeds, stood Aelthar. His dark robe fluttered in the sudden gust, eyes sharp, scanning the lake. He had arrived silently, as always, his presence both comforting and alarming.

“What is happening?” Selunara asked, her voice barely more than a whisper.

“The Black Lotus,” he said, his tone grim. “It spreads faster than we anticipated. It taints what is pure. Even the lake... it is not safe anymore.”

Selunara’s hand went to her chest, feeling the pulse of the lotus mark. “I can feel it,” she murmured. “Like a shadow creeping over my senses... first a whisper, then a weight.”

Aelthar stepped closer, keeping a careful distance. “It will worsen if left unchecked. You must stay vigilant—and trust no one outside this village for now.” His eyes softened as they met hers, though the warmth was fleeting, hidden beneath his usual calm. “I will protect you.”

They both turned to the lake. The dark veins beneath the silver surface were spreading, tendrils reaching toward the edges where reeds grew, curling as if alive. The water itself seemed to shiver in fear—or perhaps it was the corruption coursing through it.

Selunara knelt at the edge, the lantern casting long shadows across the rippling surface. She wanted to step closer, to reach out and touch the water, but instinct stopped her. The lotus mark pulsed again, sending a warmth up her arm, a silent signal from the magic she had yet to understand.

“You feel it because of the mark,” Aelthar said quietly. “The Moon’s blessing... or curse. It awakens you, makes you sensitive to the shifts of this world. Soon, you will understand the cost of that awareness.”

A sudden tremor rippled through the earth, small but unmistakable. The reeds swayed violently, and from the darkness, the faintest whisper of laughter echoed—cold, distant, and cruel. Selunara’s heart clenched.

“I... I don’t want this,” she whispered, her voice breaking. The lotus mark flared faintly, a heartbeat of light in the darkness.

“I know,” Aelthar said, his hand hovering near hers but not touching. “No one does. But fate is already moving. You must learn to face it, or the world you know will disappear.”

The wind carried a chill that seeped into Selunara’s bones, and for the first time, she understood the weight of the prophecy she had glimpsed in dreams. Shadows were spreading, not just in the lake, but in the world beyond the village, and she was at the center of it all.

Aelthar’s eyes never left hers, silent reassurance and warning intertwined. “Rest now, and do not venture far. Tomorrow, we will act. The corruption grows stronger, and so must your understanding. The Black Lotus will not wait, and neither can we.”

Selunara nodded, though unease still clenched her heart. As they turned back toward the village, the lake's surface rippled once more, dark veins curling in patterns that hinted at malice beyond comprehension. The moonlight reflected faintly on her lotus mark—still small, still pulsing—but growing, calling her to a destiny she could no longer ignore.

Chapter 7

Journey to the Healing Kingdom

The first rays of dawn painted the horizon in muted shades of gold and rose, but the village seemed draped in unease. Selunara packed a small satchel with essentials, her lotus mark faintly pulsing beneath her hair as if urging her forward. Today, she would leave the safety of the village for the first time since her awakening.

Aelthar waited at the edge of the forest, the dark folds of his cloak blending seamlessly with the morning shadows. His expression, unreadable yet commanding, softened ever so slightly as he watched her approach.

"The path is treacherous," he said quietly. "And not just because of what lies on the road. The corruption spreads, and the Black Lotus does not rest."

Selunara adjusted the strap of her satchel, her heart tight but resolute. "I have to see it, Aelthar. If the lake is a warning, the Healing Kingdom... I need to know what has been lost."

They moved swiftly through the forest, the air heavy with the scent of damp earth and wildflowers. Birds had fallen silent, and the usual chatter of small creatures was absent. Even nature seemed to sense the encroaching darkness.

As they reached the edge of the ruined kingdom, the sight stole Selunara's breath. Where she had expected orderly gardens and tranquil ponds, there was only devastation. Blackened earth stretched in jagged patterns, and ghostly remains of once-vibrant flora clawed toward the sky. The Healing Kingdom, a place she had only known in faint memory and dreams, had been hollowed out, corrupted beyond recognition.

Aelthar's jaw tightened. "Liuyin's work," he said, voice low and bitter. "She left her mark everywhere. The Black Lotus feeds on life and hope alike."

Selunara knelt by a scorched lotus pond, the petals blackened and curling inward. She touched one, feeling the pulse of death and decay, yet beneath it, a faint heartbeat of life lingered. The lotus mark on her brow pulsed stronger, and she felt a tug, subtle but insistent, pulling her toward the ruins.

"I can feel it," she whispered. "Even here... it's like the land is crying."

Aelthar stepped closer, placing a hand lightly on her shoulder. "That is why you must learn control. Your mark resonates with the Black Lotus, yes—but it also has the power to heal. You must understand that. The cost will be heavy, but you cannot ignore it."

They moved through the ruins, each step revealing more corruption: shattered shrines, twisted trees, and faint traces of ritualistic patterns burned into the ground. Selunara's heart ached at the sight, but her determination only grew.

"Look," she said, pointing to a faint glow in the distance. A single white lotus remained, untouched by the darkness, its petals gleaming faintly in the morning light.

Aelthar's eyes softened, just for a moment. "The first spark of hope," he murmured. "Even in the deepest shadow, something pure can survive. You will need to find many like it if we are to restore balance."

Selunara reached out, touching the petals gently. The warmth of the living lotus seeped into her fingers, spreading through her chest, and for a fleeting moment, she felt connected—not just to the flower, but to the moonlight, to Aelthar, and to the destiny that awaited her.

But even as she breathed in the fragile scent of hope, the wind shifted. Dark whispers rustled through the ruins, carrying the faintest echo of laughter—cold, cruel, and familiar.

"The Black Lotus is patient," Aelthar said grimly. "And it knows where your heart is most vulnerable. Remember that, Selunara. Every step forward is a choice. One misstep, and all could be lost."

Selunara nodded, determination blazing in her eyes. The journey had begun, and the Healing Kingdom had shown her both the stakes and the power that lay within her. The lotus mark pulsed stronger than ever, a heartbeat of warning, promise, and awakening.

The path ahead was uncertain, darkened by shadows and fear, but Selunara knew one thing for certain: she would not turn back.

Chapter 8

Whispers of the Raven

The night carried a chill that even the moonlight could not warm. Selunara rested in a small clearing at the edge of the ruined Healing Kingdom, her lotus mark glowing faintly beneath her hair as she drifted between sleep and dream. Her senses hummed with residual power, heightened by the corruption she had witnessed earlier, and every shadow seemed alive with whispers.

A rustle in the trees startled her awake. Perched silently upon a low branch was a raven, black as midnight, its eyes glinting with unnatural intelligence. Selunara instinctively stepped back, but the bird's gaze held her still.

"It is not just your eyes," a voice murmured in her mind. Startled, she realized the words were not spoken aloud—the raven spoke directly to her spirit. "It watches. It waits. It knows who walks among shadows."

Selunara's heart thumped, fear and curiosity warring within her. "Who... are you?" she whispered.

The raven tilted its head. "I am the watcher. I have seen what lies beyond. The Black Lotus grows stronger, and the one who unleashed it is nearer than you believe. She waits in the

Dungeon of Sorrow, weaving ruin from behind stone and shadow."

Selunara's chest tightened. Liuyin. The name came unbidden, carrying with it echoes of dreams she had not fully understood. "The Black Lotus... it's her doing?"

"Yes," the raven replied, hopping closer. "Her jealousy, her hunger for power, her bitterness... it infects the world. You, child of the moon, are both target and hope. The paths of fire and shadow converge upon you."

From the corner of her eye, Aelthar emerged silently from the trees, as though summoned by the raven's presence. His dark eyes studied the bird, then flicked to Selunara. "You have seen it?" he asked, voice low but tense.

Selunara nodded, still trying to process the revelations. "It spoke... of Liuyin. Of the Black Lotus. And... something about me."

Aelthar stepped closer, his hand brushing her shoulder lightly—not for comfort, but for grounding. "Everything the raven says is true. Liuyin's influence stretches far and wide. The corruption you sensed at the lake, the ruin of the Healing Kingdom... it is all her doing. And she will not stop until she has consumed everything she envies."

Selunara swallowed hard. The weight of destiny pressed down on her chest. "Then what do we do?" she asked. "How can I... how can we fight something that seeps into the world like this?"

Aelthar's gaze softened, but the intensity never left his eyes. "We begin by understanding it. By knowing its source, its patterns. And by trusting that your mark—the lotus—can help us counter it. But first... we must find the remnants of what remains untouched. Those pockets of life and purity are rare, yet they will guide us. The White Lotus you saw earlier was one such spark. There will be others."

The raven cawed sharply, as if confirming his words. Then it rose, wings slicing through the air, and vanished into the darkness. The warning lingered, and Selunara felt the weight of unseen eyes watching them still, noting every step, every heartbeat.

Aelthar extended his hand. "Come. There is no time to linger. The longer we wait, the stronger her influence becomes. If we move carefully, we may yet uncover her plans—and protect what can still be saved."

Selunara hesitated for only a moment before taking his hand. The pull between them, subtle yet undeniable, surged stronger. The bond forged in quiet trust, in shared fear, and in the promise of protection deepened, though neither fully understood it yet.

As they moved through the shadows, the faint glow of her lotus mark pulsed with the rhythm of hope and warning. The path ahead was fraught with danger, and the whispers of the raven echoed in her mind: *The Black Lotus watches. The world is fragile. You are the balance.*

And somewhere far beyond, Liuyin's bitter laughter rippled through the stones of her prison, a dark melody that promised ruin for those who dared oppose her.

Chapter 9

The Moon's Fading Light

The village slept under a pale, waning moon, but Selunara's rest was uneasy. A heaviness pressed upon her senses, as though invisible hands were squeezing her hearing, dimming the sharpness of the world around her. The lotus mark on her brow pulsed faintly, almost pleading, and she awoke with a start.

Aelthar stood silently in the doorway of her small cottage, his dark silhouette framed by the moonlight. Even in stillness, he radiated vigilance, a quiet storm ready to move at a moment's notice.

"You've been restless," he observed, his voice low, a mixture of concern and controlled frustration. "The Black Lotus has begun to take hold. You can feel it, can't you?"

Selunara nodded, her hands trembling slightly. "It's... my hearing... I can barely hear the wind, the birds... even your voice feels distant." She paused, swallowing hard. "Aelthar... I feel it in my chest. Like something is hollowing me out from the inside."

He stepped closer, the weight of unspoken knowledge heavy between them. "The curse drains your senses sequentially.

First hearing, then sight, then touch... eventually, the spirit itself. The Moon Empress sealed you for your safety, but the seal is weakening. You are nearing the threshold of awakening, but also of suffering."

Selunara's gaze fell to the floor, her small hands clenching in quiet despair. "Why must it be this way? Why me?"

Aelthar's eyes softened, but his tone remained firm. "Because you are the balance. Without you, the Black Lotus will consume not just this village, or the Healing Kingdom, but everything that remains pure in the mortal and celestial realms. Your suffering is part of the path. I cannot stop it, but I can help you endure it."

Her lotus mark pulsed stronger, warmth radiating across her brow. A small spark of courage ignited within her despite the creeping darkness. "Then teach me," she whispered. "Teach me how to fight it... how to protect those who cannot protect themselves."

He nodded, a rare, brief smile flickering across his face. "I will. But the path will demand more than courage. You will need to trust your instincts... and me. The cost of hesitation may be higher than you imagine."

Outside, the wind carried faint whispers, shadows dancing across the walls, echoing the corruption that had spread through the Healing Kingdom. Selunara felt the first real pang of fear, not just for herself, but for everything she loved.

Aelthar placed a steadying hand on her shoulder, the warmth of his presence grounding her. “Rest now, Selunara. Gather strength. Tomorrow, we move forward. The Black Lotus will not wait, and neither can we.”

Selunara closed her eyes, the lotus mark glowing faintly in the darkness. She could hear nothing, feel little, but a single truth resonated in her heart: she was not alone. And in that fragile comfort, she allowed herself the slimmest hope.

As the moon drifted behind clouds, dimming the night even further, Selunara’s mark pulsed with a quiet promise. The path ahead was dark, dangerous, and uncertain—but the light of her awakening, however faint, would not be extinguished.

✦ ☾ ✦

Chapter 10

The Echo of Forgotten Flames

The forest lay in hushed twilight, shadows stretching and bending as if alive. Selunara followed Aelthar through the narrow, winding paths, her lotus mark faintly pulsing with every step. Though her senses remained partially dulled by the Black Lotus's creeping influence, she felt the presence of something greater ahead—a resonance that called to the hidden depths of her soul.

Aelthar's dark cloak swept across the undergrowth, his movements precise, deliberate. He did not speak, yet Selunara sensed the weight of his thoughts: calculations, worries, and a deep, unspoken fear for her safety.

They reached a clearing where the remains of a forgotten shrine rose like spectral silhouettes against the dimming sky. Burned pillars bore inscriptions of flame and moonlight entwined, symbols lost to time. A soft, humming resonance pulsed from the altar at its center—a faint echo of power that belonged both to fire and to moonlight.

"This is the place," Aelthar whispered, kneeling at the edge of the shrine. His fingers brushed the ground, tracing the ancient sigils. "The echo of the Forgotten Flames... an artifact of old magic. It has the knowledge we need, but it is not without cost. It answers only those who are willing to risk themselves."

Selunara approached the altar, her steps tentative. Her lotus mark glowed steadily, reflecting the rhythm of the shrine's pulsing energy. A warmth rose from the ground, brushing her skin like a whispered memory. She could feel the echo of her celestial self stirring within her, faint but insistent, as if recognizing the ancient connection.

"How... how do I awaken it?" she asked, voice trembling.

Aelthar's gaze met hers, fierce yet tender. "You must call to it with all that you are—your spirit, your pain, your hope. But be warned: the magic will respond in kind. It may demand your strength, or even a part of your essence. Only you can decide if the price is worth the knowledge."

Selunara swallowed and pressed her hands to the altar. The resonance flared, sweeping through her like wildfire. Memories not yet hers flashed—glimpses of past lives, battles, laughter, and sorrow. Her heart raced, but she did not falter. Aelthar's presence anchored her, and together, they allowed the echoes to flow into her, filling the void left by the Black Lotus's creeping darkness.

Visions of fire and moonlight intertwined, forming patterns she could barely comprehend. Her lotus mark flared, and for the first time, she heard faint whispers—not from the forest, not from Aelthar—but from her own soul.

"The path of balance... the union of shadow and light... the key lies within you..."

Selunara gasped. "It's... telling me something. About the flame... and the moon... about me."

Aelthar's hand brushed hers. "Good. You are hearing it because you are ready. The power we seek—your awakening—must align with the echoes. Fire and moon, shadow and light, they are all fragments of the same whole. But heed this, Selunara: knowledge without control is dangerous. The Black Lotus will seek to corrupt what you awaken."

A tremor ran through the ground, and a dark wind swept across the clearing, carrying with it the scent of scorched earth and distant smoke. Selunara felt the tug of destiny more strongly than ever—the pull of a path she could not ignore, a burden she could not refuse.

She nodded, determination burning in her chest. "Then I will learn. I will endure... and I will protect what remains."

Aelthar's eyes softened, his hand lingering for a moment before he released it. "We must return soon. Each moment we linger strengthens Liuyin's hold elsewhere. But tonight... remember this, Selunara. You are not just a child of the moon. You are a beacon. And soon, the echoes will answer fully."

The wind settled. The forest exhaled. And in the quiet, Selunara felt her senses awaken just enough to hear the faint, distant hum of the world responding to her resolve.

Chapter 12

The Chains of Heaven

Aelthar knelt in the Celestial Hall, bound by the silver flames of the Chains of Heaven. Each link hummed with authority, searing both flesh and spirit, yet he remained calm, controlled. The Archon's glare bore into him, demanding submission. Every heartbeat was a test—obedience or defiance—and Aelthar's resolve did not waver.

The Moon Empress watched from her throne, pale robes shimmering in the light of the celestial lamps. Her expression was serene, yet beneath it lay the turmoil of a mother torn between duty and love. She had decreed his punishment, yet she knew the boy's defiance was not rebellion—it was protection, a choice born of a vow to safeguard her daughter.

"High Lord Aelthar," the Archon intoned, voice echoing across the hall, "you have broken sacred law. Mortal realms are forbidden for interference. Yet your actions remain... anomalously righteous. Why do you persist?"

Aelthar lifted his chin, the ember mark between his brows faintly glowing as he spoke. "Because she is worth the laws I break. Because silence will let darkness spread unchecked.

Because she is not just any mortal—she is Selunara, daughter of the Moon. And I will protect her, whatever the cost."

A ripple of shock passed through the council. The Moon Empress's lips pressed into a thin line, the slightest quiver betraying her relief and fear. Aelthar's words were truth, and truth was often too bold for celestial ears.

At that moment, the chains pulsed with divine energy, tightening, testing the boundaries of his endurance. Pain flared, yet a different sensation coursed through him—a subtle link to Selunara, distant yet unmistakable. Across realms, she felt a warmth, faint but insistent, brushing her senses even as the Black Lotus continued its insidious drain. Selunara's sight was dimmed, her hearing dulled, but her spirit stirred at the echo of Aelthar's will. *He is here. He has not abandoned me.* Her lotus mark glimmered, a beacon in the darkness that tethered her soul to his. She pressed her hand to her brow, feeling the pulse of energy, fragile yet steady.

Within the hall, the Archon's eyes narrowed. "So your defiance serves another purpose... to maintain a bond across realms. Clever, but forbidden. The Chains are meant to sever, not to bridge."

Aelthar's lips curved in the slightest smirk, though pain lanced through his body. "Then let the Chains try. My will is stronger than their fire."

The silver flames danced higher, sizzling, threatening to consume him entirely, yet he endured. Each pulse of energy, each tightening loop, sent echoes to Selunara—feelings, thoughts, warnings, and protection. She clutched at the sensations, letting them strengthen her resolve even as her senses faltered.

The Moon Empress finally spoke, her voice cutting through the tension. "High Council, the boy is bound, yet he continues to serve his purpose. Perhaps punishment alone will not suffice. Perhaps guidance is needed... for both him and the child."

Aelthar's gaze softened, recognizing the subtle mercy behind her words. He had not expected intervention, yet the balance between law and compassion was delicate, and the Empress had chosen wisely.

Selunara's body trembled as her vision dimmed further, but her spirit clung to the echo of his presence. The lotus mark shone faintly, a reminder that even in darkness, light could persist. The chains sought to break Aelthar's body, but they could not sever the bond that bridged mortal and celestial, moon and shadow.

Finally, the Archon relented, lowering the intensity of the flames. Aelthar remained bound, yet standing, resolute, a testament to endurance and love intertwined.

Across the distance, Selunara whispered, barely audible even to herself, "Aelthar... I can feel you. We will not fail."

And in the Celestial Hall, the ember mark flared brighter, a silent promise: no chain, no law, no darkness could sever what had been forged across time and realms.

Chapter 13

The Song of Falling Stars

Night had fallen over the village, painting the sky in velvet darkness. Yet above, stars streaked across the heavens like silver rivers, bright, fleeting, and urgent. Selunara lay on the grassy bank near the Sacred Lake, her body trembling as the Black Lotus continued its creeping assault. Sight dimmed, hearing dulled, yet her soul throbbed with a strange, insistent energy.

The whispers came first, faint as wind through the trees. Then a melody, soft and haunting, filled her mind—an echo not of this world. It was Aelthar.

"Selunara..." The voice carried warmth, authority, and something tender she could not yet name. Her heartbeat quickened. Even as the Black Lotus stole her senses, his presence cut through the haze like fire through shadow.

The stars above seemed to respond to the sound, shimmering in rhythm with the cadence of the call. Selunara rose, swaying slightly, reaching her hand toward the sky as if she could touch the celestial melody itself.

A figure materialized in the vision—a dark silhouette with medium-length hair in the half-up bun style, flowing robes catching the starlight. It was Aelthar, yet different. He glowed with ember-like energy, his ember mark faint but visible between his brows, connecting their spirits across realms.

"You are growing stronger," he whispered, voice echoing like both wind and flame. "Even as the Black Lotus drains you, your core endures. You must hold on, Selunara. Balance hangs by a thread."

Selunara's lips quivered. "I... I can feel you. But the darkness—" She faltered as her vision blurred, and the world seemed to tilt around her.

Aelthar extended a hand, though they were separated by space and plane. "Then let our bond guide you. Close your eyes and listen... not with sight, not with sound, but with the heart. The stars sing, and in their song, you will find the path."

As she obeyed, closing her eyes, the falling stars intensified, cascading across the sky in radiant streams. Each spark seemed to carve a map, a pattern of fire and moonlight entwined. Selunara's lotus mark pulsed in resonance with the celestial rhythm, a soft glow that touched even the edges of her failing senses.

Visions unfolded in her mind: flashes of battles past, healing light spreading through shadowed lands, glimpses of Aelthar's defiance in the Celestial Hall, and fragments of memories that did not belong to this life. She felt the truth:

their destinies were intertwined, past and present, fire and moon, shadow and light.

Aelthar's voice softened. "Falling stars do not perish—they transform. Each one carries the essence of what was and what could be. So too must you endure, and so must I. Only together can we restore balance."

A warmth spread through her chest, a tethering of hope against despair. She whispered, though no sound left her lips, "I will endure. I will not give in."

The stars above shifted, a constellation forming for a fleeting moment—a sign from the cosmos, a song written in light. Selunara understood, even if only partially. The path ahead was fraught with danger, yet it was hers to walk. And through the bond with Aelthar, she was not alone.

When she opened her eyes, the stars had faded, leaving only the quiet of night. But the echo remained, a persistent hum in her soul. The song of falling stars lingered, a promise that even in darkness, their light would guide the way.

Somewhere, far away in the Celestial Hall, Aelthar stood, still bound by the Chains of Heaven. Though his body suffered, his spirit was alight with the same song, reaching across realms, entwined with hers.

Balance teetered on the edge, the world poised between shadow and light. And for the first time, Selunara understood: destiny was not a chain to bind her, but a song to follow.

Chapter 14

The Oracle of the Abyss

The wind howled over the jagged cliffs of Cangwu Plains, carrying a chill that seemed older than the world itself. Selunara trudged forward, guided by the whisper of stars still echoing in her mind. Each step brought her closer to the Abyss Gate, the place spoken of in the White Tiger's prophecy and in the visions Aelthar had shared with her.

The land beneath her feet was scarred by ancient battles, the soil blackened, the air thick with the memory of forgotten power. Yet even amid decay, faint glimmers of moonlight danced on jagged stones, illuminating the path as though urging her onward.

At the center of the cliffs lay the Abyss Gate itself: a massive arch of obsidian that seemed to drink the light around it. From its depths came a hum that resonated with her heartbeat—a song she could not ignore. Her lotus mark flickered, signaling the surge of celestial energy that sought her attention.

Selunara approached cautiously, knowing instinctively that the trial awaiting her would demand more than strength—it required clarity of spirit and a willingness to confront truths she had long buried. As she stepped closer, the air grew heavy, charged with a presence that seemed alive.

"Selunara..." a voice rumbled from the darkness, deep and ethereal. "You have come."

Startled, she scanned the shadowed space and saw a figure emerge from the swirling black mists: the Oracle of the Abyss. Its form was neither entirely human nor entirely spirit—a shimmering being cloaked in void and starlight, with eyes that reflected eternity itself.

"You seek power, and yet power alone is not enough," the Oracle continued. "To awaken your true self, you must understand the cost. The path through the Abyss is not without sacrifice."

Selunara's chest tightened. "I... I am ready," she whispered, though the truth trembled beneath her words. "I will do whatever it takes to protect my people, my village... and to survive the Black Lotus."

The Oracle's gaze pierced her soul, as if weighing her intentions. "Many enter the Abyss seeking salvation or glory. Few leave unchanged. You will face your own fears, your own failings. Only by confronting them will you grasp the balance of moonlight and shadow, of healing and destruction."

A shiver ran through Selunara as images flashed before her eyes: visions of the ruined Healing Kingdom, the faint but growing Black Lotus curse, her moments of vulnerability and fear, and Aelthar's defiance at the Celestial Hall. She saw herself failing, alone, powerless—but she also saw herself rising, her lotus mark shining, connected to the ember light that was Aelthar.

"You carry the light of the Moon, yet shadows cling to your path," the Oracle whispered. "Will you surrender your fears, or let them bind you?"

Selunara drew a deep breath. "I will not be bound. I will embrace the light, the shadow, and the path I must walk. I will face whatever lies ahead."

The Oracle extended a hand, and the ground beneath Selunara trembled. A doorway of swirling silver and midnight opened before her, the threshold to the Abyss itself. A voice echoed in her mind, faint yet unmistakable: *Only those who dare to see themselves truly may pass. Only then will the fire within meet the moon without.*

With determination, she stepped forward. The swirling darkness wrapped around her like liquid night, yet the lotus mark glowed steadily, a tether to her spirit and to Aelthar, whose defiance and presence lingered across the distance.

As she disappeared into the Abyss, the Oracle watched silently, its eternal gaze fixed on the girl who would determine the fate of realms. The air remained heavy, charged with anticipation, for the first echoes of Selunara's trial had begun—and the song of the falling stars still lingered in the void, guiding her steps.

Chapter 15

The Mirror of Flames

The Abyss had swallowed Selunara whole. Darkness pressed against her from all sides, yet it was not complete emptiness; it shimmered with faint, molten threads of crimson and silver. The further she stepped, the more the threads thickened, coiling around her spirit like living fire. Her lotus mark glowed softly, a fragile beacon against the encroaching void.

At the center of the Abyss, a surface appeared—an immense mirror, rimmed with molten gold that pulsed with rhythm, as if breathing. It reflected nothing of the mortal world, yet when Selunara gazed into it, the image staring back was unmistakably her—but not merely her mortal form. This version radiated celestial light, flowing silver robes drifting around her ethereal figure, eyes bright with power and knowledge she had yet to claim.

The Mirror of Flames did not speak, but its presence demanded understanding. Selunara took a hesitant step forward. The reflection's gaze met hers, unwavering, expectant. Every beat of her heart seemed amplified in the mirrored space, echoing across realms.

"You are me," Selunara whispered, voice trembling, "and yet... not."

Her reflection inclined its head slightly, as if acknowledging the truth. The air thickened, warm and oppressive, carrying a scent of molten iron and moonlight. Selunara could feel the weight of power contained within the mirror—the potential of her celestial self, waiting to awaken.

Then, the whisper came—familiar, intimate, and filled with ember light. "Selunara... do not fear it. You must accept what you are, or the Black Lotus will consume all that you love."

The voice was Aelthar's, echoing through the Abyss despite the distance. Her lotus mark pulsed in response, flaring brighter, and she felt the tether that bound them grow, almost tangible. Even across realms, he had risked everything to reach her, and now his presence lent her courage.

Selunara reached toward the mirror. As her fingertips brushed the surface, ripples spread, and the reflection moved—not as a mirror but as a living, breathing version of herself. Flames of silver and crimson licked along its form, weaving together light and shadow.

"You cannot face this alone," the reflection said, voice resonant yet distinctly hers. "But guidance can be found in those who share your path. Trust him."

Selunara felt a surge of warmth, a sudden infusion of power through her lotus mark. Aelthar's voice whispered again, stronger now: "I will join you. Whatever the law, whatever the cost, I am with you."

Suddenly, the chains of distance seemed to dissolve. Aelthar stepped into the mirror with her, shadow and flame intertwining, his ember mark glowing in tandem with her lotus. Their spirits touched, merging briefly across the divide of mortal and celestial, and the Mirror of Flames responded. It shivered, cracked slightly along its golden rim, releasing sparks of energy that danced around them.

Selunara's celestial self smiled, a mirror of understanding and acceptance. "Now you begin. The fire within and the moon without—they are one. Step beyond fear. Step beyond hesitation. Only then can the path forward be seen."

She inhaled deeply, letting the warmth of their joined spirits fill her. The Mirror of Flames was no longer a reflection—it was a threshold. And together, Selunara and Aelthar stepped forward, the Abyss bending around their awakening, forging a bridge between mortal courage and celestial destiny.

The air shimmered with energy, the boundaries of the mirror dissolving. Selunara's heartbeat steadied, her senses sharper, though still tinged with the Black Lotus's lingering shadow. For the first time, she understood the depth of her power—and the necessity of trusting both her strength and the bond that tethered her to Aelthar.

Beyond the Mirror of Flames lay new trials, new revelations, and the merging of destinies that would shake realms. But in this moment, Selunara felt whole, poised at the edge of awakening, ready to face the path that had been written for her since birth.

Chapter 16

The Children of Fire and Moon

The Abyss shifted around Selunara and Aelthar, no longer merely a dark void but a swirling nexus of light and shadow. Flames of ember intertwined with silver moonlight, casting reflections that danced like living spirits across the obsidian walls. Here, in this in-between realm, mortal and celestial blurred, and the air itself hummed with the resonance of power.

Selunara felt it first—a warmth that was neither hers nor Aelthar's alone, but something born from the union of both. Her lotus mark pulsed in tandem with the ember mark on Aelthar's brow. Each beat of their hearts sent ripples of energy through the Abyss, and the Mirror of Flames behind them shimmered, reflecting not one but two sets of childlike forms: ethereal manifestations, innocent yet radiant, born of fire and moon.

"They are... our children," Selunara whispered, awe in her voice. The child-spirits mirrored their celestial essence, silver and crimson interwoven, eyes bright with nascent intelligence and unspoken understanding.

Aelthar's expression softened. "Not in the mortal sense... but in essence. They are the embodiment of our shared power, our bond. In them lies the future we are meant to protect." His voice was steady, yet laced with reverence.

The children moved gracefully, circling them, leaving trails of luminescence in the Abyss air. Each step they took seemed to stabilize the swirling chaos around Selunara. The oppressive weight of the Black Lotus lessened, though its shadow still lingered at the edges.

Selunara reached out to touch one of the child-spirits. It mirrored her gesture, and a wave of warmth flowed into her chest, searing away the cold despair that had taken root. In that moment, she understood the significance: their union was not merely emotional or spiritual; it was cosmic. Their combined essence was a new force capable of countering the spreading corruption.

Aelthar took her hand. "This is why the Moon and Shadow sought each other across lifetimes. Our bond... it is not chance. The prophecy was never just about survival. It is about balance, creation, and renewal."

Selunara nodded, feeling a profound calm settle over her. "Then we must learn from them, guide them... and through them, find the strength to face the trials ahead."

The child-spirits danced between them, their presence illuminating hidden paths within the Abyss. Selunara glimpsed corridors of molten light, passageways that could lead her closer to the Cangwu Seal and beyond, yet each corridor pulsed with latent danger. The Black Lotus had not been banished; it awaited, and these children—manifestations of hope and unity—were both shield and compass.

One of the spirits floated forward, smaller and more fragile than the others. It reached toward Selunara, and the lotus mark on her brow flared, bathing the child in soft moonlight. The spirit's voice, clear though unspoken, resonated in her mind: *Balance is born not from avoidance, but from courage. You and he are the bridge.*

Aelthar tightened his grip on her hand. "We are stronger together. And now, through them, we can endure the Abyss in ways neither of us could alone."

Selunara's eyes shimmered with determination. The children were not merely symbols—they were the living embodiment of their commitment, their love, and their combined destiny. Every ripple of light they left in the void reminded her: the path forward was one of unity, courage, and unwavering trust.

As the Abyss calmed around them, and the mirror behind them dimmed into the shadows from which it had emerged, Selunara and Aelthar took a step forward together. The child-spirits followed, weaving threads of fire and moonlight into the path ahead.

Somewhere in the celestial realm, the stars themselves seemed to shift, acknowledging the new balance forming in the Abyss. Selunara inhaled, letting the warmth of the children and Aelthar's presence settle into her bones. She felt ready—ready to face the trials of Cangwu, ready to reclaim the power and truth that the Black Lotus threatened to erase. In that nexus of moonlight and flame, Selunara understood a truth deeper than prophecy: love, courage, and unity could forge a power greater than any curse. And together, they would step beyond the Abyss into destiny itself.

Chapter 17

The Cangwu Seal

The Cangwu Plains stretched before Selunara and Aelthar, an endless expanse of jagged rock and silver grass swaying under a restless wind. Shadows stretched unnaturally long, as if the land itself were alive, watching, testing. The distant ruins of ancient temples whispered of civilizations long vanished, their secrets buried beneath centuries of dust and silence.

Selunara's lotus mark throbbed faintly, a reminder of both her power and the lingering curse of the Black Lotus. Aelthar's ember mark glimmered in tandem, a tether connecting them across worlds. Each step they took toward the Cangwu Seal seemed heavier, the weight of destiny pressing against them.

"The Seal lies ahead," Aelthar said quietly, scanning the horizon. "Guarded not by brute force alone, but by trials of the spirit and heart. Only those willing to face themselves—and each other—may approach it."

Selunara's gaze shifted to the horizon, where a massive stone structure rose from the plains. Its surface was etched with glowing runes, faintly pulsing with silver and crimson light.

The air around it crackled with ancient energy, and a low hum resonated through the ground.

As they approached, a sudden gust of wind carried a chorus of whispers, voices speaking in languages both familiar and alien. Shapes began to materialize from the plains: guardians of the Seal, their forms flickering between humanoid and elemental. One was wreathed in silver flames, another in shadowed mist, each moving with grace yet exuding a silent warning.

Selunara's heart quickened. "We must show them we mean no harm," she said, though her voice trembled slightly. The children of fire and moon—the manifestations of their shared essence—floated around her, illuminating the guardians with threads of light and warmth.

The silver-flamed guardian stepped forward, eyes like molten mirrors. "Those who seek the Seal must demonstrate balance. Fire and moon, light and shadow... you must share the weight, or be consumed by it."

Aelthar nodded, understanding the unspoken challenge. "We will not falter. Whatever the cost, we face it together."

The first trial began with the guardians conjuring illusions drawn from Selunara's deepest fears and regrets. She saw the ruins of the Healing Kingdom, the Black Lotus consuming the land, and faces of those she could not save. Every step forward required courage, each heartbeat a defiance against despair.

Beside her, Aelthar's presence was a steady anchor. He faced his own trials: visions of his failures, of the celestial laws he had broken, of the weight of duty that often isolated him from the world he swore to protect. The children of fire and moon mirrored both their strengths and weaknesses, guiding them through the shifting illusions.

"Trust the bond we share," Aelthar whispered. "We are stronger together."

Selunara's lotus mark flared, and a wave of energy radiated outward, stabilizing the illusions. The guardians watched silently, testing the authenticity of their unity. One by one, the illusions dissolved, replaced by clear paths leading to the central chamber of the Seal.

There, set upon a pedestal of obsidian, lay the Cangwu Seal itself—a crystalline structure that shimmered with silver light infused with ember-red veins. Its surface seemed alive, responding to their proximity. As Selunara approached, a voice echoed within her mind: *The Seal demands an anchor, a life willingly offered. Only through shared risk can balance be restored.*

She glanced at Aelthar. "It asks for a sacrifice... for someone to give themselves fully."

Aelthar's ember mark pulsed brighter. "We do not need to face this alone," he said. "Our bond, our shared power... we can anchor it together."

Selunara hesitated, then took his hand. Their combined essence, reflected in the child-spirits surrounding them, surged through the Seal. Silver moonlight and crimson flame intertwined, forming a lattice of energy that began to mend the cracks in the Seal. The Guardians observed silently, nods of acknowledgment passing between them as balance slowly returned to the ancient structure.

Yet even as the Seal stabilized, Selunara felt a pulse of warning: the Black Lotus still lingered, seeking cracks in their unity, testing the limits of their shared power. The Abyss, the Mirror of Flames, and now the Seal—each trial had strengthened them, but the greatest challenges were yet to come.

Aelthar squeezed her hand. "We are ready. No matter what lies ahead, we face it as one."

Selunara nodded, determination burning in her chest. With the Cangwu Seal stabilized, the path forward was illuminated—but the shadows of Liuyin's vengeance and the lingering curse of the Black Lotus promised trials beyond anything they had yet endured.

Together, they stepped away from the Seal, their bond stronger than ever, and prepared to face the next chapter of their destiny.

Chapter 18

The Choice Beneath the Stars

Night draped over the Cangwu Plains, a velvet blanket studded with silver stars. The wind whispered through jagged rocks, carrying a chill that seeped into Selunara's bones, yet the warmth of Aelthar's presence kept the cold at bay. Together, they had reached the outer sanctum of the Cangwu Seal, but its true trial had only just begun.

Before them rose an ancient stone dais, etched with celestial runes that pulsed with the rhythm of distant moons and embers alike. The Seal hovered above it, glowing with a combination of silver and crimson, veins of light stretching outward like veins in living flesh. A low hum vibrated through the plains, resonating with their heartbeat and magnifying every whisper of fear and hope.

Selunara knelt, hand extended toward the Seal. Her lotus mark flared, and the child-spirits of fire and moon circled them, their glow weaving between silver and crimson threads. A sudden, ethereal voice filled the night air: *To restore the Seal, a life must be given willingly. Only a heart bound in true unity can anchor the balance.*

She froze. Her breath caught in her chest. The sacrifice demanded was not vague—it required courage and total commitment, the willingness to risk oneself for the other.

Aelthar knelt beside her, his ember mark shimmering against the starlight. "Selunara... we don't have to face this alone. The Seal does not demand one over the other. We share the risk. Together." His voice was steady, filled with conviction that defied the weight of destiny pressing on them.

Selunara swallowed, her eyes searching the vast night sky as if seeking guidance among the stars. She felt the pull of destiny, heavy but clear. *This is what it means to be celestial and mortal, fire and moon, together.*

The child-spirits drifted closer, their luminous forms flickering like distant constellations. They radiated understanding, and in their silent presence, Selunara felt the courage she had feared lost. "Then... together," she whispered, her fingers intertwining with Aelthar's.

As they focused, the Seal responded. Threads of silver and crimson light coiled around them, intertwining with their essence. Pain shot through Selunara as if her soul were being stretched between the mortal and celestial planes, yet it was accompanied by a warmth that filled her heart. The Seal pulsed violently, testing their commitment, probing their fears, and weighing the strength of their bond.

Suddenly, a vision filled her mind: the Moon Empress, serene and distant, appeared above the plains, her silver robes shimmering against the starlight. Her voice, calm but commanding, resonated within Selunara: *You must choose wisely, child. Balance is delicate. Too much fear, too much hesitation... and all is lost.*

Selunara's eyes met Aelthar's. There was no fear in his gaze, only unwavering determination. *Then we will not falter,* she thought, letting their hearts beat in unison, their celestial and mortal essence merging with the Seal.

The child-spirits flared in response, weaving silver and crimson threads that anchored the Seal's power. Energy surged around them, crackling and bending the night air into shimmering arcs of light. Selunara felt the full weight of choice settle over her—the potential for failure, the cost of courage, and the promise of unity.

Step by step, breath by breath, they allowed themselves to be part of the Seal. Pain and warmth intertwined, fear and trust balanced in equal measure, until the Seal shone brighter than the stars above. Slowly, the humming of the plains softened, and the night air stilled. The Cangwu Seal had accepted their shared commitment.

Selunara opened her eyes, her lotus mark glowing faintly but steadily. The child-spirits hovered around them, radiating calm. Aelthar's hand tightened around hers, ember mark bright but gentle now, a mirror of her serenity.

“We did it,” Selunara whispered, a tremor of relief in her voice. “Together.”

Aelthar nodded. “The choice was never just about life or death. It was about unity... about trusting what we are, what we can become together.”

Above them, the stars seemed to shimmer in approval. The Seal pulsed once, then settled, stable and whole. But even as relief washed over them, both knew the Black Lotus still lingered, a shadow at the edge of their path. Their trials were far from over.

Selunara looked to Aelthar, determination blazing in her eyes. “Then we move forward. Whatever comes next, we face it together.”

He smiled faintly, a rare softness breaking through his brooding demeanor. “Together,” he agreed.

And under the canopy of stars, fire and moon intertwined, anchoring the balance, ready to face the unfolding destiny that awaited them.

Chapter 19

The Silent Bloom

The night had fallen over the plains, yet an unnatural stillness lingered. Even the winds seemed to hold their breath, as though waiting for something inevitable. Selunara sat upon a flat stone, her hands folded in her lap, lotus mark faintly glowing between her brows. The child-spirits of fire and moon hovered silently around her, their soft light illuminating her face, but even they could not chase away the creeping dread she felt.

Something within her had shifted. The triumph of the Cangwu Seal had come at a cost she could feel deep in her bones. Her senses—once vibrant—were dulling, subtle at first, almost imperceptible. She noticed the faint echo of silence in the wind, the dulled shimmer of starlight, the muted fragrance of silver grass. Each loss was a whisper, but together they formed a silent cry of warning.

Aelthar knelt beside her, placing a hand gently over hers. His ember mark shimmered softly, a protective pulse in the darkness. "Selunara... your mark is fading again," he said quietly. His voice carried both concern and urgency. "The Black Lotus... it is reaching further than we imagined."

Selunara met his eyes, trying to mask the fear she felt. "I thought the Seal would stabilize everything... that our shared strength would protect me." Her voice was a fragile thread against the silence. "But I can feel it... something is still wrong."

Aelthar tightened his grip, his resolve unwavering. "It's never gone. Liuyin's influence spreads like a shadow, subtle but deadly. You are not weakened because of yourself—you are being tested. And we will face it, as always... together."

The child-spirits flitted around them, responding to the tension in the air. Their soft glow illuminated traces of black veins in the grass—a sign that the curse of the Black Lotus had begun to manifest here, even in this sacred space. Selunara's chest tightened, her heartbeat echoing the silent bloom of the creeping corruption.

"I... I can't hear it fully anymore," she whispered, the first sign of sensory loss manifesting in her mind. The whisper of wind, the faint call of distant creatures—everything was muffled, hollow. Panic surged for a moment, but Aelthar's presence steadied her.

"You can still feel it," he said. "Not with ears, not with eyes, but here." He placed his palm over her chest. "Let your heart guide you. Trust the bond."

Selunara closed her eyes, focusing inward. The child-spirits circled faster, their movements synchronizing with the rhythm of her pulse and Aelthar's. In that unity, she felt a faint warmth bloom where fear had taken root. A bloom of hope, fragile yet defiant. The Silent Bloom, she realized, was the slow emergence of resilience amidst creeping darkness.

A sudden whisper split the stillness—a voice, neither fully human nor divine, carried on the wind: *The Black Lotus thrives on isolation. Protect the heart, and the bloom survives.*

Selunara's eyes flew open, meeting Aelthar's unwavering gaze. "We can't let it take me," she said, determination hardening her tone. "We must find the source... before it spreads beyond the plains."

Aelthar's ember mark pulsed brighter. "Then we begin tonight. I will leave no stone unturned, no secret unexplored. Liuyin has hidden far too long, but we will find her. And we will end this before it reaches you completely."

The child-spirits swirled around them, their glow now steady, a protective cocoon in the darkness. Selunara drew a slow, calming breath, letting the warmth of Aelthar's presence, the children's glow, and the certainty of their shared bond anchor her.

"The Silent Bloom is not an end," she whispered. "It is a beginning. And we will face it together."

The wind sighed through the plains, carrying with it the faint fragrance of silver and fire. Somewhere in the distance, the first hints of Liuyin's machinations stirred, the shadows of revenge spreading quietly. But Selunara, strengthened by love, unity, and the courage born of trials, was ready to meet whatever awaited.

Together, she and Aelthar stepped forward, the child-spirits guiding their way, as the Silent Bloom began its quiet yet relentless rise.

Chapter 20

The Dungeon of Sorrow

Deep beneath the Moon Palace, a place untouched by sunlight, lay the Dungeon of Sorrow. Its walls were carved from black stone, slick with moisture and etched with ancient runes designed to suppress magic. Shadows clung to every corner, whispering the regrets and malice of centuries. This was where Liuyin had been confined—a punishment for her obsession and envy—but confinement had only sharpened her wrath.

Liuyin sat cross-legged in the center of her cell, her silver robes now streaked with black veins of corruption. Her beauty had not faded, yet it carried a hardness, an edge born from isolation and rage. The air around her crackled faintly with the latent power she nurtured, growing stronger with every passing day.

"They think they can contain me," she murmured, voice low but seething. "They think the Chains of Heaven, the Dungeon's walls, the Moon Empress herself can erase what I have become. They are fools."

Her fingers traced the runes etched into the stone floor, drawing energy from the residual moonlight that filtered through tiny cracks above. The Black Lotus, her creation, still thrived in distant lands, seeding corruption in silence. Each time she sensed Selunara's mark flicker or weaken, a surge of satisfaction warmed her chest. The girl was vulnerable, fragile... and the world around her ripe for the chaos Liuyin could unleash.

From the shadows, a figure emerged—a small wisp of dark energy, the messenger she had sent to test the Cangwu Seal. "Mistress," it whispered. "The Seal was touched... but only shared. They survive... for now."

Liuyin's amber eyes narrowed. "Only for now. They have tasted power, and it has made them bold. But even boldness has limits. The Silent Bloom they cherish so dearly... I will pluck it before it fully rises."

She rose gracefully, the black veins in her robes writhing like living ink. "This dungeon is a prison for the body, not the mind. Soon, the Moon Empress will regret every decision she made to keep me contained. Soon, every plan they make, every step they take... will fall into my hands."

Beyond the Dungeon, the moonlight flickered across the distant Cangwu Plains, illuminating the child-spirits circling Selunara. Liuyin could sense them, faint threads of energy betraying their location. Her smile widened, dark and predatory. "The girl thinks she can grow strong. Let her. Let her rise as high as she dares... and then watch as I shatter every piece of her world."

She extended her hand, fingertips glowing faintly. Black tendrils seeped from her mark, weaving intricate patterns in the air. With each stroke, the tendrils spread across the void beyond her cell, reaching into distant lands where the Seal and the Silent Bloom had begun to flourish.

"The Moon's daughter will learn the true cost of defiance," Liuyin whispered, her voice carrying through the dungeon like a curse. "And when she does... she will beg for a mercy I will not grant."

Even as the echoes of her threat faded into the black stone walls, the Dungeon of Sorrow vibrated subtly, a testament to the malice and power contained within. Liuyin sank back onto the cold floor, eyes closed, already weaving the threads of her next scheme. Every moment Selunara and Aelthar drew breath was a moment closer to the reckoning she had long awaited.

Above, the wind whispered across the Cangwu Plains, carrying with it a faint chill—the promise of trials yet to come, and a darkness that would test the bonds of fire and moon like never before.

Chapter 21

The Moon's Lament

The moon hung low over the village, its pale light spilling across rooftops and silvering the tops of the trees. Yet beneath its serene glow, a sorrowful weight pressed upon the night. Selunara sat at the edge of the Sacred Lake, her hands cupped in the cool water, feeling the faint pulse of moonlight ripple through her fingers. But the more she tried to sense the world around her, the more muted it became. The Black Lotus was relentless, quietly stealing her connection to the senses she had once taken for granted.

Iryndor knelt beside her, his healer's robes brushing against the ground. He had been her steadfast companion through the trials, her anchor in a world that seemed increasingly distant. His eyes reflected worry, shadows of fear she could not hide even if she tried. "Selunara," he said softly, "you cannot face this alone. Let me help you—please."

Selunara turned her head slowly, a faint smile tugging at her lips despite the tremor in her chest. "I know you are here, Iryndor. That is my strength... for now." But even as she spoke, a small tremor of panic rippled through her. The sounds of the night—the rustle of leaves, the distant call of a nightbird—were fading, replaced by a haunting silence.

Meanwhile, far from the village, Aelthar moved swiftly through shadowed forests and across jagged cliffs, his senses attuned to every disturbance in the magical currents. His ember mark glowed faintly beneath his dark hair, pulsing in time with his concern for Selunara. He carried with him the weight of her fading senses and the knowledge that the Black Lotus could spread beyond the plains if left unchecked.

He paused atop a ridge, gaze sweeping over the moonlit valley below. The wind carried whispers—traces of the curse—but it was faint, like the ghost of a memory. He clenched his fists. "Selunara," he murmured, voice swallowed by the night. "Hold on. I will find the Tears of the Moon. I will restore what is being stolen from you... and no darkness, no matter how deep, will take you from me."

Back at the lake, Selunara raised her hands, letting the faint glow of her lotus mark mingle with the pale light of the moon. She could feel the tug of something distant, a faint pulse of ancient magic—the hint of the Tears hidden somewhere beyond reach. She knew, instinctively, that her survival, her awakening, and the restoration of the Seal depended on their recovery.

Iryndor placed a steadying hand on her shoulder. "You will not face this alone. Aelthar is searching. And together..." His voice faltered as he sensed the fragility of her spirit. "Together, we will endure."

Selunara closed her eyes, letting the remaining fragments of her senses focus inward, drawing on the warmth of their presence. The Black Lotus had stolen much, but it had not yet taken the essence of her spirit. The Silent Bloom, she realized, was still alive within her, fragile yet unyielding.

Above, the moon shivered behind a thin veil of clouds, its light a silver lament across the water. Selunara whispered, almost to herself, "Moon... guide him. Protect him as he protects me. And let me endure until he returns."

Somewhere, in the distance, a faint echo of movement stirred the night. Aelthar's journey was far from over, but the threads of destiny were converging. Moonlight and ember, shadow and lotus, love and duty—all intertwined.

Selunara opened her eyes, resolve burning in her gaze despite the creeping loss. "I will not falter," she murmured. "I will wait... and I will rise."

The lake rippled softly under the night sky, reflecting the determination of a girl whose senses might fade but whose spirit remained indomitable. The Moon's Lament was heavy, yes—but within it lay the promise of hope, of reunion, and of the trials yet to come.

Chapter 22

Ashes of the Healing Kingdom

Aelthar moved through the remnants of what had once been the Healing Kingdom, his boots crunching on ash and charred stone. The air was thick with the scent of smoke and decay, a bitter reminder of Liuyin's subtle but relentless vengeance. Trees that had once flourished with silver leaves were blackened and brittle, and the sacred waters of the Healing Lake now reflected only gray shadows.

The village healers' shrines had been reduced to rubble. Broken crystals, scattered herbs, and scorched scrolls littered the ground. Even the smallest signs of life—the songbirds, the fluttering butterflies—had vanished, as if the very air had been drained of vitality.

Aelthar knelt by a lone, blackened lotus, its petals still clinging stubbornly to the stem despite the devastation. His ember mark glowed faintly, reacting to the residual energy of the Black Lotus that had overtaken the land. The small flower seemed almost to pulse in silent protest, a whisper of life amidst ruin. He bent closer, his breath heavy with grief and fury.

"This..." he murmured, brushing ash from the lotus petals. "This is the work of Liuyin. Her curse is stronger than we imagined. But she underestimates us. Always."

He reached out, letting a fraction of his shadow energy mingle with the flower, stabilizing it against the lingering corruption. The small pulse of restored vitality gave him hope—a sign that even in devastation, life could endure.

A faint sound made him freeze. Soft, deliberate footsteps echoed across the ruined stones, distant but deliberate. His hand went to the hilt of his blade, eyes scanning the ruins for movement. "Show yourself," he commanded, voice low but sharp.

From the shadows, a figure emerged—a messenger, cloaked in darkness yet unmistakably Liuyin's creation. The wisp-like being bowed low. "Master Aelthar... the Black Lotus spreads beyond the Healing Kingdom. Selunara's senses are faltering faster than predicted. She relies on you now more than ever."

Aelthar's jaw tightened. "I know," he said, eyes narrowing as he scanned the horizon. "The girl's strength is not enough alone. Every step I take brings me closer to her... and to stopping Liuyin's corruption before it consumes more."

He rose, his cloak fluttering in the wind that carried the smell of ash and the faint glow of the moon. His mind raced—there were clues here in the devastation, remnants of magic left behind by the healers, the scattered energies of the Cangwu

Seal, and traces of Liuyin's signature dark influence. Every fragment told a story, every flicker of energy was a warning.

As he moved deeper into the ruined kingdom, he discovered the lone white lotus, standing defiantly amid the ruin. Its petals gleamed faintly under the moonlight, pure and untainted by the Black Lotus. Aelthar's breath caught.

"This is it," he whispered. "The sign... the proof that Liuyin's power can be undone."

He knelt, extending his hand. The lotus responded, a gentle warmth spreading through the air, faintly illuminating the ruins around him. Energy flowed from the flower, forming a subtle path of magic he could trace—a trail left intentionally, perhaps by the healers or by fate itself.

"This trail..." he murmured, realizing the significance. "It leads to the Tear of Aelora. That is our next step. We cannot falter now, not while Selunara's life and the balance of the realms hang in the balance."

The wind stirred, carrying ash and faint whispers from the past. The ruined Healing Kingdom was silent once more, but within its ashes, hope endured. The lone white lotus stood as a beacon, fragile yet unbroken, just like Selunara herself.

Aelthar rose, determination blazing in his eyes. He would follow the path, recover the Tear, and face whatever darkness awaited. Nothing—neither Liuyin's schemes nor the creeping shadows—would stop him from protecting Selunara.

The ruins faded behind him as he pressed onward, the faint glow of the lone white lotus lighting the first steps of a path that would lead them both toward the trials yet to come.

Chapter 23

The Curse Unveiled

The wind carried a bitter scent as Aelthar approached the threshold of the Dungeon of Sorrow. The black stone walls loomed like silent sentinels, heavy with centuries of contained malice. He had followed the faint trail left by the lone white lotus, every step bringing him closer to the source of the devastation that had stolen Selunara's senses.

Inside, Liuyin's aura pulsed with raw, unrestrained power. The veins of black magic that had twisted her robes now writhed like living shadows, responding to her fury. She was no longer merely an imprisoned goddess; she was a force of corruption, sharpened by isolation and jealousy.

"You come at last," Liuyin's voice rang out, dripping with venom and amusement. "I wondered how long it would take for the brave protector to follow the breadcrumbs I left for him."

Aelthar stepped forward, his ember mark faintly glowing beneath his dark hair. "Liuyin," he said evenly, voice calm but edged with authority. "Enough games. I know the truth now. You created the Black Lotus. You poisoned the Healing Kingdom. You've been manipulating Selunara's senses to weaken her, to make her vulnerable."

Liuyin's laugh was a sharp, broken sound that echoed through the dungeon. "You think you understand?" she sneered. "Do you have any idea what it is to be ignored, cast aside, watched while others are exalted? I loved... and was denied. I desired... and was overlooked. The Moon Empress herself, with her precious daughter, thought she could hide what was meant to be mine! The Black Lotus is my justice, my art, my vengeance!"

Aelthar's eyes narrowed, his heart heavy with both anger and sorrow. "Your jealousy does not justify this. Innocent lives suffer because of your obsession. Selunara is not a pawn for your vengeance."

Liuyin's amber eyes blazed, the dark veins around her mark pulsing like living fire. "Pawn? No. She is the proof of what I could not have. She is the vessel through which the Moon Palace's arrogance will taste ruin. And you... you were foolish enough to follow her trail, thinking you could stop me."

Aelthar's shadow energy flared around him, his cloak billowing as he stepped closer, unwavering. "I will stop you. I will undo this curse if it's the last thing I do. Selunara's life—and the balance of the realms—depend on it. Your schemes end here, Liuyin."

For a moment, the dungeon was still, the air thick with the tension of power poised on the brink. Liuyin studied him, curiosity flickering through her rage. "You dare defy me? Even after breaking the laws of heaven to protect her?"

"I do," he said firmly. "Because some laws are meant to serve life, not destroy it. And because I will not let your bitterness determine the fate of the girl I protect."

A faint tremor ran through the dungeon, as if the walls themselves shivered at the confrontation. Liuyin's hands glowed with a black fire, coiling outward like serpents seeking freedom. "Then face me," she whispered, "and witness the power you've challenged."

Aelthar drew on his own reserves, his shadow energy intertwining with the faint embers of flame within him. A silent pulse resonated between their marks—the lotus and the ember, the clash of moonlight and shadow. He sensed the depth of her schemes now, the precise reach of the Black Lotus, and the danger it still posed to Selunara.

"This ends now," he said, voice low and unwavering. With a surge of concentrated power, he projected a barrier, isolating Liuyin's energy from reaching beyond the dungeon's walls. The shadows shrieked in response, the black veins writhing violently as if resisting the containment.

Liuyin's laughter broke through the magical hum. "Contain me if you can, protector. But know this—my curse is already in motion. Even if I am imprisoned, the Black Lotus will continue to bloom, and the Moon's daughter will pay for the arrogance of her birth!"

Aelthar's gaze hardened. "Then we will follow every thread, undo every taint. I will not fail her. Not now. Not ever."

As he stood, the dungeon seemed to pulse with the latent energy of Liuyin's hatred, but beneath it all, a faint, stubborn flicker of life persisted—the promise that, though darkness had spread, it could be countered, unraveled, and healed. Aelthar would see to it.

The Curse had been unveiled, its origin exposed. And with that knowledge came the first glimmer of hope: understanding the enemy's design meant that Selunara's strength, though waning, could be restored—and the path to redemption, though fraught with danger, was now clear.

Chapter 24

The Fading Light

Selunara sat by the small hearth in her village home, her fingers tracing faint patterns on the wooden table. The light of the fading evening sun mingled with the dim glow of the fire, casting soft shadows across her delicate features. But within her, a growing emptiness gnawed at her senses. Hearing had dulled, colors seemed muted, and the warmth of the hearth felt distant, as if separated by an invisible barrier.

Iryndor knelt beside her, hands trembling slightly as he examined her. "Selunara... your senses are fading faster than I anticipated," he said, voice heavy with concern. "We need Aelthar. Only he can reach the source of this—only he can restore you."

Selunara tried to speak, but her voice came out barely above a whisper. "I... I can't rely on anyone too much," she murmured. Her eyes, dimmed but still luminous, met his. "I have to endure this... until he returns."

Iryndor shook his head, frustration mingling with fear. "Endure? Selunara, you're slipping away. The Black Lotus doesn't just steal your senses—it takes your connection to life itself. You can't fight this alone."

Her gaze faltered, and she swallowed hard, fighting the growing panic that threatened to overwhelm her. She had always been strong, always had a light within her—but now that light flickered dangerously close to being snuffed out.

At that moment, a shadow stirred near the doorway. Selunara's head turned instinctively, and though her sight was dim, she felt the familiar pull of Aelthar's presence. Relief surged through her, mingled with fear—he had come, but what would he find? What could he do against the creeping darkness of the Black Lotus?

Aelthar knelt beside her, his dark robes brushing the floor, ember mark faintly glowing as he extended his hand. "Selunara," he murmured, voice steady yet filled with urgency. "You're not alone. I've traced the source. The path to the Tear of Aelora is open, and we can restore your senses. But we must act quickly—the Black Lotus spreads with every passing moment."

Selunara reached for his hand, her fingers barely brushing against his. A faint warmth passed between them, enough to anchor her, enough to remind her of life beyond the creeping darkness. "I... I trust you," she whispered, voice trembling. "But it's so hard... everything feels distant."

Aelthar's gaze softened, though it held steel beneath the tenderness. "I know. I feel it too. But together, we will fight this. I will not let it take you from me."

Iryndor stepped back, bowing slightly, but his eyes were wary. "Aelthar... be careful. Selunara's condition is worsening. If the Black Lotus spreads any further..." He left the threat unspoken, but its weight hung heavily in the room.

Selunara's lotus mark glimmered faintly between her brows, pulsing in rhythm with her slowing heartbeat. She could feel her connection to the world fraying—hearing, sight, touch, spirit—all slipping like sand through her fingers. But the warmth from Aelthar's presence was a lifeline, fragile but steadfast.

"Then let us not waste time," Aelthar said firmly. "We move at dawn. I will lead the way to the Tear of Aelora. And I swear... your senses, your spirit—they will be restored."

Selunara nodded, a mix of hope and fear in her expression. "I will hold on... for you, for life, for... everything." Her voice faltered as the last remnants of sound around her grew faint, yet the determination in her heart remained.

As the night deepened, the hearth's glow flickered and the shadows stretched long across the floor. Selunara's senses may have been dimming, but her spirit burned brighter than ever. And somewhere beyond the horizon, Aelthar prepared to embark on the perilous journey that would either save her—or confront them both with the true darkness of the Black Lotus.

Chapter 25

Shadows of Redemption

The air in the Shrine of Aelora was thick with ancient magic, a dense, almost tangible energy that pressed against Aelthar as he stepped across the threshold. The shrine had long been abandoned by mortals and celestials alike, considered too dangerous, too sacred, and too unpredictable for any who sought its power without cause. Now, Aelthar walked its halls with purpose, guided only by the faint pulse of the Tear of Aelora.

Every step echoed softly against the marble floors, each sound amplified in the stillness. Shadows danced along the walls, cast by the flickering torches he had ignited. They seemed alive, moving as if watching, waiting for a misstep. He kept his hand on the hilt of his sword, but he knew the weapon alone would not be enough. This was a place of trial, of testing, where the boundaries between light and shadow blurred.

"Selunara's life depends on me," he whispered to himself, the ember mark between his brows glowing faintly. The warmth of her presence lingered in his mind, fragile yet persistent, guiding his steps. "I cannot fail her. Not after everything."

As he advanced deeper, the shrine's corridors twisted unnaturally, as if the walls themselves were alive. Faint whispers curled through the air, remnants of past supplicants who had sought redemption or power. He ignored them, focusing on the faint shimmer ahead—the Tear of Aelora, hidden in the heart of the shrine, guarded by ancient wards that had repelled even the strongest of celestials.

Suddenly, the shadows thickened. Black tendrils of magic seeped from the corners, coiling toward him, carrying the unmistakable signature of Liuyin's dark influence. Though she remained imprisoned in the Dungeon of Sorrow, her power had begun to leak outward, tainting even this sacred space.

"Liuyin..." Aelthar muttered, tightening his grip. "You are bound, yet you reach beyond your chains. But I will not falter."

The tendrils lunged forward, and Aelthar met them with shadow energy, his flame-imbued aura repelling the encroaching darkness. The clash of powers sent a shiver through the shrine, walls cracking and dust falling like rain. He could sense the immense strain of keeping the black magic at bay, and he knew that each second wasted would bring Selunara closer to irreversible harm.

He pressed forward, reaching the inner sanctum where the Tear of Aelora floated within a prism of light. Its radiance was gentle yet unwavering, a pure silver glow that seemed to hum with the rhythm of the moon. Aelthar stepped closer, feeling the pull of the Tear as if it called specifically to him, or perhaps to the girl he protected.

But just as his fingers brushed the surface, a voice echoed through the chamber—cold, calculating, and filled with malice. "You dare approach what I could have touched? You dare challenge me, protector?"

The shadows twisted violently, and Liuyin's essence appeared in spectral form, reaching from her prison. Her eyes burned with obsession, her presence radiating the weight of centuries of envy and power denied. "The Tear could be mine," she hissed. "And with it, Selunara will know despair unlike any she has felt. Her senses, her mind, her soul—everything will belong to me!"

Aelthar stepped into the silver light, letting his ember mark flare brighter, creating a protective shield around himself. "You are bound, Liuyin. Your reach may be long, but it ends here. Selunara will not fall to your hatred."

The spectral figure lunged, striking with a force born of envy and desperation. Shadows and light collided, sending waves through the chamber. Aelthar's body moved with fluid precision, deflecting and countering, but he could feel the drain on his energy. Every strike, every ward, brought him closer to exhaustion. Yet he could not stop, could not allow Selunara to remain weakened.

Finally, with a final surge of combined shadow and ember energy, he severed Liuyin's reach, forcing the spectral form to retreat into the prison where it belonged. Panting, Aelthar knelt before the Tear, lifting it carefully. Its light pulsed against his chest, a reassurance that Selunara's restoration was now within reach.

The journey back would be perilous, but the first step toward redemption had been taken. The shadows of Liuyin's wrath still lingered, but hope had returned—a single beacon in the darkness. Aelthar's resolve solidified: he would heal Selunara, reclaim her senses, and face whatever consequences the Moon Empress or the heavens might impose.

The Tear of Aelora hummed gently, a promise that, despite the shadows, there remained light. And as Aelthar emerged from the Shrine of Aelora, the first glimmers of dawn broke through the horizon, casting long silver rays across the world—an omen that the fight to restore life, love, and balance was only just beginning.

✦ ☾ ✦

Chapter 26

The Moon's Requiem

The night was silent, broken only by the whispering wind that swept across the high cliffs overlooking the village. Aelthar moved swiftly, the Tear of Aelora cradled in his hands, its silver light pulsating like a heartbeat. The journey back to Selunara was urgent; every second she remained weakened, the Black Lotus claimed a little more of her senses, her spirit, her very connection to the world.

Yet the path was not clear. Liuyin's influence had not been entirely contained. As he descended the cliffs, shadows slithered across the ground, subtle but menacing. The black veins of her magic, though weakened, still sought to reach him, to reclaim the Tear for her vengeance. Aelthar's ember mark glimmered with a protective flame, each pulse a warning, a shield, and a promise.

He paused atop a ridge, the moonlight spilling silver across his dark robes. He closed his eyes briefly, letting the Tear resonate with his own inner energy. A soft hum filled the air, and he felt a flicker of Selunara's presence—the faint stirrings of life, of awareness, fragile but undeniable. She was reaching out in the darkness, and he had to meet her halfway.

Below, in the village, Selunara stirred in her modest home. The darkness that had clouded her senses now seemed to pulse with a mournful rhythm, like a lament woven by the moon itself. Her hands clutched the edge of the table, and for a moment, she felt a warmth—an echo of Aelthar's presence. "I... I remember him," she whispered, her voice barely audible. Her lotus mark glimmered faintly, a tiny beacon in the shadow of her fading senses. Flashes of past moments—a protective hand, a familiar gaze, a shared smile—danced behind her eyes. Though incomplete, the memory was enough to stir hope, enough to anchor her to life.

Meanwhile, Aelthar reached the village outskirts. The ground beneath him seemed to vibrate faintly, a warning of Liuyin's lingering malice. Yet he pressed forward, every step guided by the growing pulse of the Tear and the fragile thread connecting him to Selunara.

Inside, Iryndor noticed a subtle shift. "She's responding," he whispered, awe mingled with concern. "The Tear... it's reaching her, even from afar."

Selunara's vision, though still dim, caught the faint silver glow seeping from the horizon. She felt the presence of someone—no, someone strong, unwavering, and protective. Her fingers twitched, reaching for what she could not yet see. And in that moment, a melody of memory and longing intertwined—the Moon's Requiem.

It was not just a song; it was an echo of her celestial self, a hymn carried by the moonlight to awaken what remained of her senses. The darkness that had claimed her faltered, retreating in the presence of this resonant energy. For the first time in days, she could hear the faint rustle of leaves, the crackle of the hearth, and, most importantly, the distant but unmistakable thrum of Aelthar's approach.

Aelthar finally entered her home, the Tear held aloft. Its light bathed her in silver warmth. "Selunara," he said softly, kneeling beside her. "I am here. I have brought the Tear. You are not alone."

She reached toward him instinctively, her fingers brushing the glow of the Tear. A rush of sensation coursed through her—hearing, sight, touch—all returning in rapid, exhilarating waves. Her lotus mark shone brightly now, fully awakened, reflecting the silver light of the Tear.

"I... I feel..." she breathed, astonished, tears welling in her restored eyes. "Everything... it's coming back."

Aelthar's hand enveloped hers, his ember mark flaring softly against her restored glow. "Yes, Selunara. The Moon's Requiem calls you back. The darkness cannot hold you. We will restore balance together."

Outside, the night wind carried a gentle chorus, as if the moon itself had acknowledged the return of its child. And though Liuyin's presence still lingered, restrained within her dungeon, the first victory had been won. Selunara's senses had returned, and with them, a renewed strength—and a bond with Aelthar that would now shine brighter than ever against the shadows that threatened their world.

The Moon's Requiem had been sung, and its melody promised that even in the depths of despair, light would always find a way.

Chapter 27

The Fire of Reunion

Dawn broke over the village, soft silver rays spilling across rooftops and fields, but inside Selunara's home, a different kind of light pulsed—a warm, golden glow that mingled with the lingering silver of the Tear of Aelora. The air vibrated with energy, alive with the unspoken promise of reunion and the weight of destiny.

Aelthar knelt before Selunara, the Tear floating between them, radiating a delicate balance of power. His ember mark flared with intensity, reflecting his determination. "Selunara," he whispered, voice steady yet trembling with emotion, "it is time. Together, we can restore what was lost and awaken what has long been dormant."

Selunara's fingers brushed his, the touch sending sparks through her being. The restored senses were nothing compared to the power now swirling between them—the merging of fire and moonlight, shadow and silver, past and present. Her lotus mark pulsed brightly, responding to his ember, and for the first time, she felt the connection that had always bound them, even before memories returned.

"Your power... your presence..." she murmured, eyes wide as visions flickered behind her eyelids. Memories long buried—

whispers of a life before, moments of love, laughter, and tragedy—came rushing back. She saw herself in celestial robes, standing beside a dark figure whose eyes were filled with devotion and quiet sorrow. Aelthar.

"Yes," he said softly, pressing his hand against hers. "It is us. I am here. Always. Through lifetimes, through trials, I have sought you. And now, the balance can be restored."

The Tear of Aelora pulsed brighter, resonating with their union. Energy surged, weaving silver moonlight and ember fire into a radiant aura that enveloped them both. The walls of the village seemed to shimmer, reality bending gently under the magnitude of their merged powers. Shadows that had lingered in corners and under rooftops recoiled, unable to withstand the harmony of their reunion.

Selunara gasped as the final pieces of her past life aligned. She remembered Aelthar's vow, the sacrifices made, the moments lost to fate and time. And most vividly, she remembered the love that had always existed between them—a love that defied gods, realms, and curses alike.

Tears streamed down her cheeks, not of sorrow, but of relief, awe, and joy. "I remember... us," she whispered. "Everything. I remember why... we must be together."

Aelthar pulled her close, letting their energies entwine fully. The Tear of Aelora's glow bathed them in warmth, reinforcing the bond that had transcended centuries. Within that union, their powers combined into a force neither mortal nor fully celestial—a new essence, bridging worlds, reshaping fate.

From this fusion, the first signs of Eclipsera appeared: a shimmering in-between realm, ethereal and delicate, created by the merging of their celestial energies. Two child-spirits, glowing faintly, emerged from the radiant aura, representing the union of moon and flame. They circled the pair in gentle, protective arcs, their tiny forms flickering with curiosity and light.

Selunara looked at Aelthar, awe mingled with wonder. "Is this... real?" she asked, her voice quivering with the weight of revelation.

He smiled softly, brushing a strand of her hair from her face. "It is real. The Fire and the Moon, united at last. Our bond has not only awakened you but created something new—something the heavens have never seen. And now, we can face what comes next, together."

A tremor shook the ground outside, faint but undeniable. The balance of heaven itself had been touched by their union, a warning that the forces opposing them would not remain idle. Yet within the home, in this moment, Selunara and Aelthar were whole, their love reaffirmed, their purpose clear.

"I've waited for this," she murmured, resting her head against his chest, feeling the warmth of the ember mark against her lotus glow. “All my life... every life... waiting for you.”

“And I,” he said, voice filled with reverence, “have sworn to protect you through every darkness. Now, together, we will set the world right.”

The first light of dawn filtered through the window, mingling with the ethereal glow around them, a sign that even as heaven quaked at their union, hope and love endured. The Fire of Reunion had been ignited—and nothing, not even the shadows of Liuyin’s malice, could extinguish it.

Chapter 28

The Last Gate

(The Final Trial)

The skies above the ruined plains churned with unnatural darkness. The air trembled as if the world itself feared what was to come. At the center, a swirling vortex of shadow and fire clawed its way toward reality—the Hell Gate. Liuyin's magic, unbound and twisted by centuries of envy and hatred, pulsed with destructive intent.

Selunara and Aelthar arrived at the edge of the vortex, their merged powers radiating outward in a brilliant aura of silver moonlight and ember fire. The child-spirits of Eclipsera hovered around them, tiny beacons of hope and balance in the gathering chaos.

"Liuyin..." Selunara's voice rang, steady yet laced with fury. "It ends here. You will not destroy the world for your vengeance."

Liuyin's form materialized within the maelstrom, her white robes now darkened with black veins that writhed like living shadows. Her eyes burned with obsession. "You think your petty union can stop me? I have endured centuries of neglect, rejection, and humiliation. Now, I will have my revenge! The Hell Gate will open, and all will kneel before my power!"

Aelthar stepped forward, his ember mark glowing fiercely. "You were given punishment and a chance for redemption, Liuyin. You chose hate. And for that, the balance you threaten will be undone."

The ground quaked beneath their feet as the vortex expanded, swallowing the landscape in a choking blend of flame and shadow. Selunara lifted her hands, lotus mark shining brilliantly, and summoned the full strength of her lunar powers. The air around them shimmered as their energies intertwined, forming a radiant barrier that pushed back the dark vortex.

But the Hell Gate's pull was relentless. From the swirling chaos, visions of Kael's mother—the true orchestrator behind centuries of strife—emerged. Her form, veiled in shadow, radiated black magic that rivaled even Liuyin's wrath. It was she who had unleashed curses, manipulated fate, and fueled the Black Lotus that had nearly consumed Selunara.

Aelthar's jaw tightened. "So this was her hand all along... Mother." His voice trembled, not with fear, but with the weight of betrayal. "You manipulated everything, even me."

Selunara's eyes narrowed. "We face her now, whatever her power. Together, we stop this. The world cannot be broken."

Liuyin screamed, a high, piercing sound, and surged toward them. Shadow tendrils lashed out from her body, meeting the combined force of Selunara's lunar light and Aelthar's ember fire. Each strike of darkness met a counter of brilliance, sparks flying, energy colliding, shaking the heavens themselves.

"You will pay for centuries of torment!" Liuyin shrieked, her magic warping the very ground, opening fissures that belched shadow flame.

Selunara and Aelthar moved in perfect unison, their powers flowing as one. She struck with beams of silver that burned through the shadow, while he channeled flames that seared through darkness. Together, they created a cyclone of light and heat that held Liuyin at bay.

But the Hell Gate's pull remained. From its depths, monstrous forms writhed—twisted remnants of souls corrupted by black magic. Selunara's heart ached as the images of innocent lives appeared, some she remembered from the Healing Kingdom, others faceless and crying. She could not let them fall.

Aelthar placed a hand over hers. "We share this burden," he said firmly. "Our union is stronger than any shadow. Channel with me."

With synchronized breaths, they poured every ounce of their essence into the Tear of Aelora. The aura flared, a brilliant bridge of moonlight and fire stretching toward the swirling

Hell Gate. Shadows shrieked and twisted, Liuyin's form wailing as she was drawn back toward the Dungeon of Sorrow, restrained by the combined force of their power.

The vortex convulsed violently, then, with a deafening roar, began to collapse in on itself. Black flames sputtered and dimmed, shadow tendrils retracting, screaming into nothingness. The Hell Gate, the culmination of Liuyin's vengeance and Kael's mother's manipulation, imploded, leaving only scorched earth and a quiet, trembling wind.

Selunara sank to her knees, exhausted, lotus mark dimming as she drew in a shaky breath. Aelthar knelt beside her, ember mark faint but steady. "It is done," he whispered. "The world is safe—for now."

Liuyin's form faded into the Dungeon, her fury contained but her hatred eternal. And in the distance, Selunara glimpsed the shadow of Kael's mother retreating, her plans thwarted but her presence a looming reminder that the battle for balance was never fully over.

Selunara looked up at Aelthar, eyes shining with tears and relief. "We did it. Together."

"Yes," he said, pulling her close. "Together, always."

And as the first true light of morning bathed the plains, a fragile peace returned—a peace born of fire, moonlight, and an unbreakable bond that had defied time, fate, and the shadows of vengeance.

Chapter 29

When the Moon Wept Fire

The heavens trembled. Stars flickered as if holding their breath, and the moon hung low, bleeding silver light across the scarred plains. The aftermath of the Hell Gate's collapse left the world fragile, a trembling canvas for the final confrontation. Though Liuyin was restrained and the immediate threat neutralized, remnants of her dark magic lingered, festering like embers in the wind.

Selunara and Aelthar stood together atop the highest ridge, their hands intertwined, their combined energy—a fusion of moonlight and ember fire—radiating outward. The Eclipsera child-spirits circled them, tiny symbols of hope, balance, and the future that had been forged from centuries of struggle.

Yet the world was not yet free. From the shadows, Kael's mother emerged, her form wreathed in black magic that had festered through generations. The force she commanded was immense, born from centuries of greed for power and the desire to control the celestial and mortal realms alike. Her eyes, cold and unforgiving, fixed upon Selunara.

"You think a child's light and a shadow's fire can stop me?" she sneered, her voice like steel cutting through the night.

"All that you love, all that you cherish, will crumble before my will."

Aelthar stepped forward, ember mark blazing, shadowed robes rippling in the celestial wind. "You are wrong," he said firmly, voice carrying the weight of unyielding devotion. "The bond we share—Selunara and I—is stronger than any darkness you wield. We protect life, love, and balance. That is power you will never understand."

Selunara's lotus mark shimmered brilliantly, reflecting the moonlight and responding to the fire in Aelthar's mark. The air around them thrummed with energy, a tangible harmony that pushed against the lingering dark magic. "Your hatred ends tonight," she said softly, yet with the authority of a goddess reborn. "We will not let your shadow consume this world."

Kael's mother unleashed a torrent of black energy, hurling shards of corrupted magic toward them. The Eclipsera child-spirits spun rapidly, creating a protective barrier of light around Selunara. Aelthar channeled his power alongside hers, the silver and ember merging into a brilliant storm that collided with the darkness in a cataclysmic explosion.

The ground quaked violently, fissures splitting the earth, black flames licking the edges. Lightning, both silver and fiery red, tore through the sky. Selunara and Aelthar moved as one, their bond flawless in execution, weaving counterattacks with precision, each strike dismantling the intricate web of Kael's mother's magic.

Liuyin, still trapped but partially reaching out with lingering malice, screamed as her power clashed with their combined force. Yet it was Selunara who sensed the pivotal moment—the precise thread where Kael's mother's spell could be undone if she and Aelthar poured everything into one final, decisive act.

"Aelthar," she whispered, determination flaring in her eyes, "together, now. Everything we are, everything we have—pour it into the world."

He nodded, placing his hand over hers once more. "With you, always."

Energy surged, the fusion of lunar light and ember fire expanding outward, enveloping the battlefield in a dazzling glow. The dark magic screamed, twisted, and contorted, then shattered like glass, leaving only echoes of its malevolence. Kael's mother's figure wavered, her black magic dissolving, her voice cracking with disbelief and fury.

But the cost was immense. Selunara felt her essence waver, a portion of her celestial power being consumed in the effort. Aelthar's shadow flame flickered and dimmed, his body trembling under the strain. They had succeeded, yet the victory demanded sacrifice—a reminder that even gods and demi-gods are not immune to the cost of restoration.

As the dust settled, the moon hung serenely in the sky, its silver light washing over the battlefield. Selunara collapsed into Aelthar's arms, exhausted but alive, her lotus mark dimmed yet still radiant—a quiet testament to the balance restored.

Aelthar held her close, whispering, "It is done. The world is safe, Selunara. The Moon has wept fire tonight, and through it, we endured. Together."

Selunara looked up at him, tears of relief streaming down her cheeks. "And we... we are still here. Together."

The celestial war had ended. The Hell Gate remained closed, the darkness subdued, and the bonds of love, sacrifice, and courage had ensured the survival of all that mattered. In the distance, the first signs of a renewed world began to emerge—green shoots of life reclaiming the scarred plains, the faint warmth of sunlight returning to the horizon, and the soft, reassuring glow of the moon watching over all.

For Selunara and Aelthar, the Fire of Reunion had led them through the final trial. The heavens themselves had trembled, but the promise of balance and love endured, a legacy written in fire, moonlight, and unbreakable devotion.

Chapter 30

Eternal Twilight

The village lay bathed in a calm twilight, the horizon a gentle blend of amber and silver. Life had begun to heal, both in the land and in hearts. The scars of the celestial battles—the Hell Gate, the Black Lotus, the ruins of the Healing Kingdom—had left their marks, but the pulse of renewal ran strong beneath the soil, through the rivers, and in the skies.

Selunara walked slowly through the familiar streets, dressed in simple mortal clothes, her long hair falling loosely with delicate buns, the lotus mark between her brows faint but visible when the light caught it. Children ran past, their laughter like music, and villagers greeted her with warm smiles. For the first time in years, she felt completely at peace.

Aelthar followed her, moving quietly yet with a presence that demanded attention. His dark robes, though simpler than in his celestial guise, retained a subtle shimmer of silver and ember. The ember mark between his brows glowed faintly, a quiet reminder of the power he had shared and sacrificed to protect the world—and her.

They reached the old oak at the center of the village, a place that had been their sanctuary in both mortal and celestial trials. Aelthar took her hand gently, his touch grounding her after centuries of turmoil. “It feels... strange,” he murmured, “to be here, knowing the world is safe. That we are safe.”

Selunara smiled, her fingers brushing his. “It is strange, yes... but it is home. For the first time, I feel like I truly belong. Not just to a realm or a prophecy, but to this life, to you, and to peace.”

A soft glow appeared in the distance. The moon, full and serene, cast its silver light across the village, reflecting in the river like molten glass. From the heavens, a gentle warmth settled over them, a blessing from the Moon Empress herself. Though she had erased Selunara from celestial records to protect her, the bond between mother and daughter endured.

Aelthar’s voice was soft. “Have we truly left the shadows behind?”

Selunara leaned against him, eyes lifting to the twilight sky. “Shadows will always exist... but so will the light. We have chosen it. Together, we carry both fire and moon, balance and love. That is more than enough.”

In the distance, the faint glimmer of the Eclipsera child-spirits danced among the trees, unseen by others but ever present as a symbol of the bond between moonlight and ember fire. Life had resumed its rhythm; laughter, work, and the quiet rituals of daily living filled the air. The world had endured, and so had they.

From the shadows of the village, Iryndor watched with satisfaction, knowing his duty to protect Selunara had reached its natural end. The healer's heart was heavy with relief and pride. Around the outskirts, traces of the past—fissures, scorched earth, and faint echoes of celestial magic—reminded all that sacrifices had been made. But they were a testament to the courage, love, and choices of those who had fought for a brighter tomorrow.

Selunara lifted her gaze to Aelthar, eyes shimmering with quiet tears. "Let us walk forward," she said, voice steady, "without fear, without shadows lingering over our hearts. Our story... is ours now."

Aelthar nodded, drawing her close. Together, they stepped into the twilight, hand in hand, their hearts intertwined. The ember and the lotus glowed faintly, a gentle reminder that the fire and the moon would always exist within them, guiding their path.

Above, the moon shone like a guardian, watching over a world now free from vengeance and darkness. Stars sparkled faintly, as if nodding in approval at the choices made, sacrifices given, and love rekindled.

The world was not perfect, but it was theirs. And in that eternal twilight, Selunara and Aelthar found what they had sought across lifetimes: peace, balance, and a love that transcended worlds.

Author's Note

Thank you for walking beside Selunara and Aelthar through moonlit trials, shadowed choices, and the fire of destiny. This story was born from my love of celestial mythology and the belief that love survives lifetimes.

May this book stay with you long after the last page fades.

— **Deepali**

About the Author

Deepali is a visionary storyteller who blends celestial mythology, Asian-inspired fantasy aesthetics, and emotional romance to create powerful, immersive worlds. Her stories explore destiny, love, and the delicate balance between moonlight and shadow.

Follow Deepali online:

- Website: lotussutrabooks.com
- Instagram: @author_deepali
- Goodreads: Author Deepali

Also, by Deepali

- *Messages from Angels*
- *Everyday Healing Practices*
- *The Minimalist Lifestyle Reset*

...and more to come.

www.ingramcontent.com/pod-product-compliance
Lightning Source LLC
Chambersburg PA
CBHW062142160726
48282CB00027B/907
* 9 7 8 9 3 3 4 4 2 0 2 9 6 *